Play with "e" and "d"

Library of Congress Cataloging-in-Publication Data
Moncure, Jane Belk.
Play with "e" and "d" / by Jane Belk Moncure ; illustrated by Colin King.
p. cm.
Summary: A brief tale emphasizing the uses
of "e" and "d" in various words.
ISBN 1-56766-934-4 (library bound)
[1. Alphabet—Fiction.]   I. King, Colin, ill. II. Title.
PZ7.M739 Pe 2001
[E]—dc21
00-010844

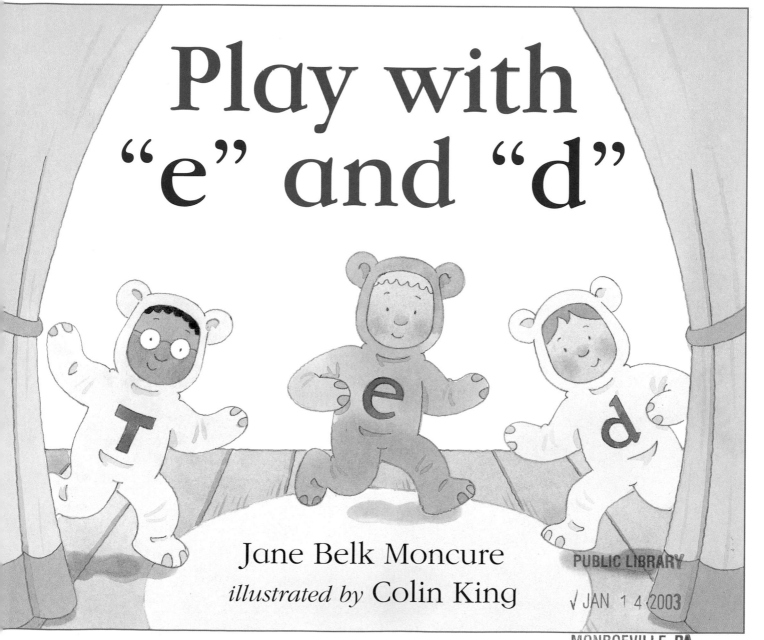

Play with "e" and "d"

Jane Belk Moncure

illustrated by Colin King

Starring the letters...

and

The publisher wishes to thank the letters "e" and "d."
Without them this book would not be possible.

This is little e.

This is little d.

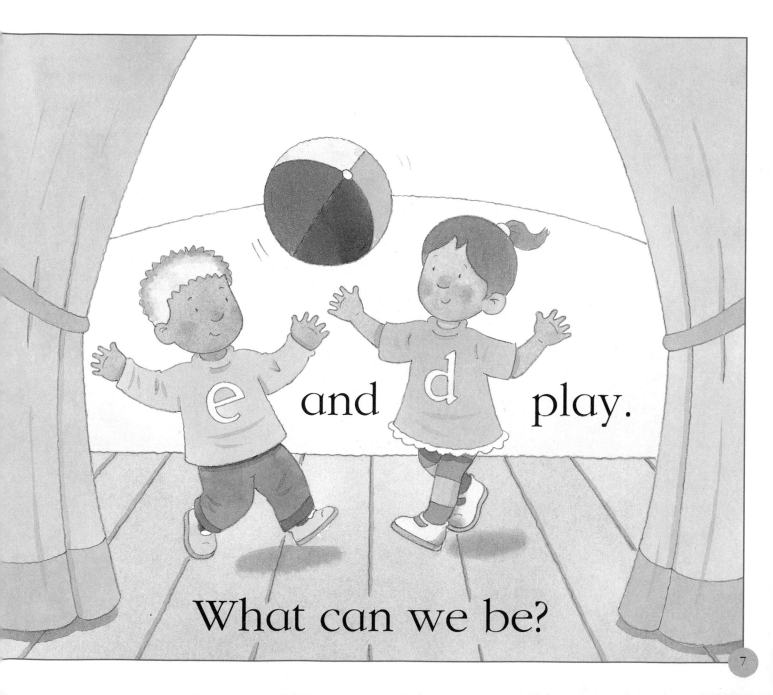

e and d play.

What can we be?

This is big

May I play?

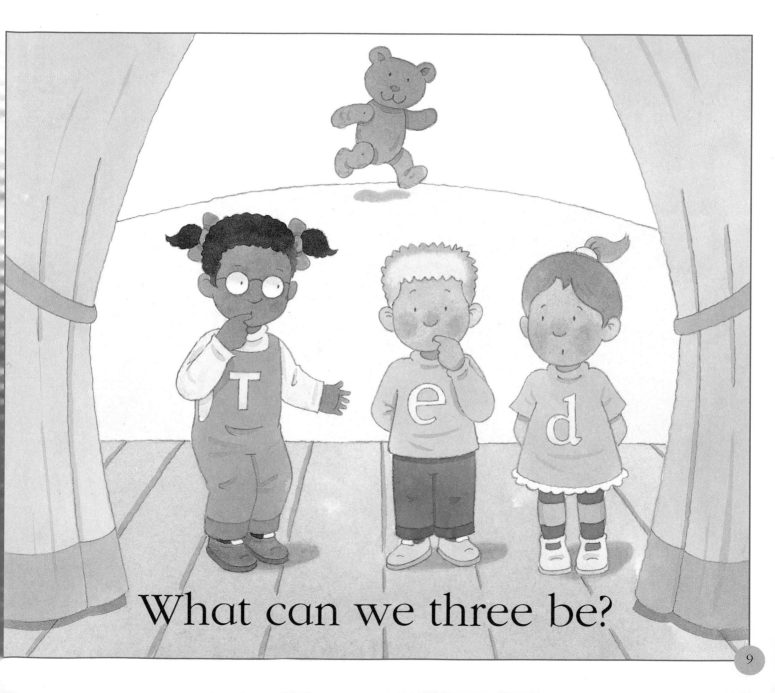

What can we three be?

Ted. This is Ted.

Do what Ted can do.

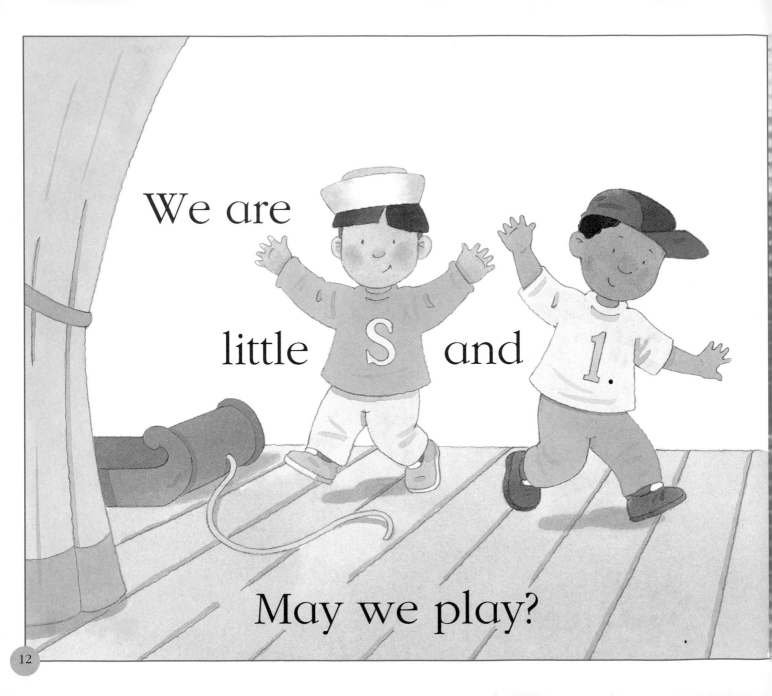

We are little S and 1.

May we play?

12

What can we four be?

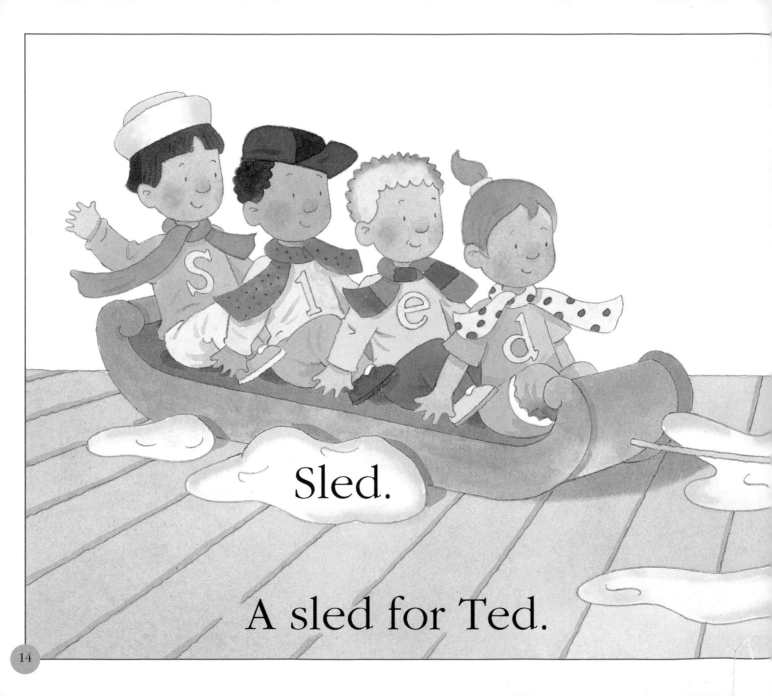

Sled.

A sled for Ted.

Ted, Ted, pull the sled.

Pull the sled, Ted!

Look out!

What is that?

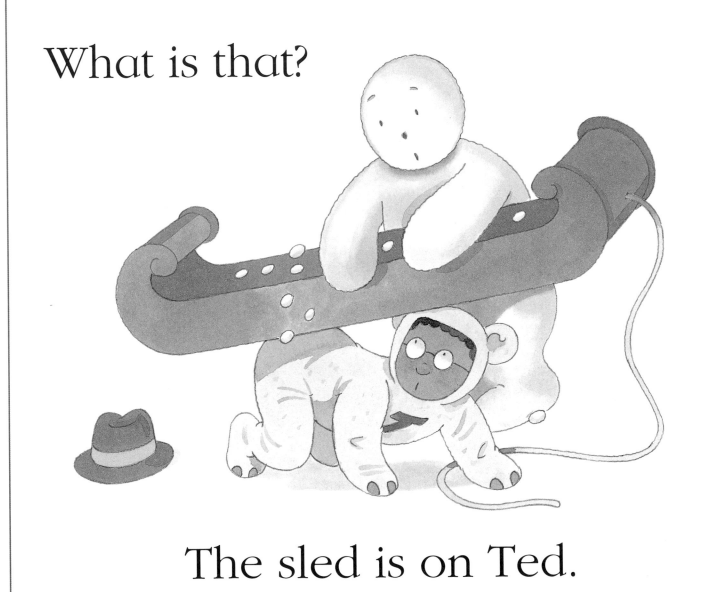

The sled is on Ted.

Ted is on the sled.

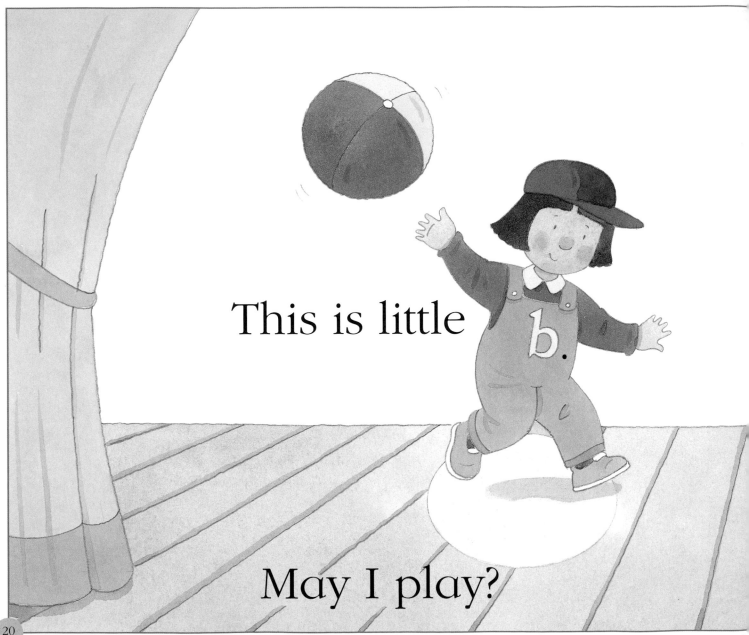

This is little b.

May I play?

What can we three be?

21

Bed. A bed for Ted.

Ted is in bed.

Where is the sled?

The sled is under the bed.

Get the sled, Ted.

Ride the sled, Ted.

Good-bye, sled.

Good-bye, bed.

Good-bye, Ted.

and

also play with

30

and

and

Can you?

ABOUT THE AUTHOR AND ILLUSTRATOR

Jane Belk Moncure began her writing career when she was in kindergarten. She has never stopped writing. Many of her children's stories and poems have been published, to the delight of young readers, including her son Jim, whose childhood experiences found their way into many of her books.

Mrs. Moncure's writing is based upon an active career in early childhood education. A recipient of an M.A. degree from Columbia University, Mrs. Moncure has taught and directed nursery, kindergarten, and primary grade programs in California, New York, Virginia, and North Carolina. As a former member of the faculties of Virginia Commonwealth University and the University of Richmond, she taught prospective teachers in early childhood education.

Mrs. Moncure has travelled extensively abroad, studying early childhood programs in the United Kingdom, The Netherlands, and Switzerland. She was the first president of the Virginia Association for Early Childhood Education and received its award for outstanding service to young children.

A resident of North Carolina, Mrs. Moncure is currently a full-time writer and educational consultant. She is married to Dr. James A. Moncure, former vice president of Elon College.

Colin King studied at the Royal College of Art, London. He started his freelance career as an illustrator, working for magazines and advertising agencies.

He began drawing pictures for children's books in 1976 and has illustrated over sixty titles to date.

Included in a wide variety of subjects are a best-selling children's encyclopedia and books about spies and detectives.

His books have been translated into several languages, including Japanese and Hebrew. He has four grown-up children and lives in Suffolk, England, with his wife, three dogs, and a cat.